ALSO BY ANNA ALTER

Sprout Street Neighbors: A New Arrival

Sprout Street Neighbors: Five Stories

A Photo for Greta

Disappearing Desmond

Abigail Spells

SPROUT STREET
NEIGHBORS

Bon Voyage

BOOK 3

ANNA ALTER

A YEARLING BOOK

All rights reserved. Published in the United States by Yearling, an imprint of Random House Children's Books, a division of Penguin Random House LLC, New York.

Yearling and the jumping horse design are registered trademarks of Penguin Random House LLC.

Visit us on the Web! randomhousekids.com

Educators and librarians, for a variety of teaching tools, visit us at RHTeachersLibrarians.com

Library of Congress Cataloging-in-Publication Data
Names: Alter, Anna.
Title: Bon Voyage / Anna Alter.
Description: New York : Alfred A. Knopf, 2017 . |
Series: Sprout Street neighbors ; [3] |
Summary: Mili loves her new home but misses the excitement of traveling, so she persuades her neighbors to join her on a trip to Paris.
Identifiers: LCCN 2016030795 (print) | LCCN 2016058139 (ebook)
ISBN 978-1-5247-0053-9 (pbk.) | ISBN 978-1-5247-0054-6 (lib. bdg)
ISBN 978-1-5247-0055-3 (ebook)
Subjects: CYAS: Neighbors—Fiction. | Voyages and travels—Fiction.
Apartment houses—Fiction. | Animals—Fiction. | Paris (France)—Fiction.
France—Fiction. | BISAC: JUVENILE FICTION / Social Issues / Friendship.
JUVENILE FICTION / Animals / General.
Classification: LCC PZ7 .A4635 Bon 2017 (print)
LCC Pz7.A4635 (ebook) | DDC
[Fic]—dc23

The text of this book is set in 14-point Perrywood.
The illustrations were created using pen and ink with acrylic.

Printed in the United States of America
10 9 8 7 6 5 4 3 2 1
First Yearling Edition 2017

For all brave explorers

CONTENTS

CHAPTER 1

The Map

Mili looked as small as an ant next to the Great Pyramid. It stretched so high over her head, you couldn't see the top in the photograph. Mili's eyes twinkled. She set her photo album down and reached into a cup on her desk. Then she turned to her map and placed a red pin in the city of Giza, Egypt.

She opened her album again. This time, she stopped at a picture of giraffes on an African plain. The sunset glowed orange behind them,

casting long shadows at their feet. Mili remembered the warm sunlight on her fur and the tall grass waving in the breeze. She picked up a blue pin and placed it in the country of Botswana.

She returned to her photos. "Mmm," she said, gazing at a photo of herself nibbling sweet mochi in a bustling Japanese market. She reached into the cup again and placed a green pin in the city of Kyoto.

Mili stepped back to get a good look. The map was a rainbow of pins, tracing her travels all over the world.

But when she glanced around her apartment at 24 Sprout Street, the world felt small.

The faucet dripped. Dishes slept in the cupboard. Her books lay dusty on the shelves. "Everything is the same as it was yesterday," she thought. "And it will be the same way tomorrow."

She picked up her photo album, flipping through the pages. *SWISH.* A piece of paper slipped from the book and sailed to the floor. It was an old magazine clipping with a picture of the *Mona Lisa,* the most famous painting in the world. Mili had always wanted to see it in person. It sat in a museum in Paris, France.

Mili got an idea. She toppled off her chair and across the hall to Emma's apartment. *Tuk-tok.*

"Come in!" called Emma.

Mili walked into the living room.

5

Emma's legs and tail were sticking out from under the couch cushions and waving wildly.

Emma popped her head out. "Don't mind me! I've lost my lucky socks. I know they're in here somewhere!" She pulled a fork out of the cushions and tossed it onto the floor. Then she stuck her head back in the sofa.

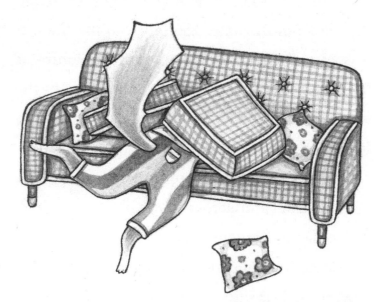

"Emma," said Mili softly, "would you like to go on a trip?"

Emma's tail flipped back and forth. "A WHAT?" shouted Emma from under the cushions. "A SHIP?"

Mili cupped her paws around her mouth. "A TRIP!" she shouted back.

Emma poked her head out of the couch again. "Can you pass me my magnifying glass?"

Mili spied the glass on the desk and handed it to Emma.

"Thanks," said Emma, crawling deeper into the sofa.

Emma seemed far too busy to go anywhere. So Mili headed downstairs.

Tuk-tok.

"Hi, Mili," said Henry at his door. "Could you lend me a hand?"

"Sure," said Mili, following him into the kitchen.

Henry handed her a picture of a sailboat. Then he climbed a ladder and hammered a nail into the wall. Mili handed him the picture, and he hung it on the nail.

"Is it straight?" he asked.

"I think so," answered Mili.

"Great," said Henry. "A tidy home is a happy home."

Mili cleared her throat. "Henry, would you like to go someplace new?"

"Why would I do that?"  he snapped. "Everything I need is right here."

Henry's eyes

8

darted across the kitchen. "Except for sand-wiches," he added. "Maybe I'll head to Sergio's."

Mili said goodbye and walked across the hall. *Tuk-tok.* But no one answered. Outside, she found Wilbur weeding in the yard.

"Hi, Mili," said Wilbur, peeking out from behind an azalea bush.

"Wilbur," began Mili, "would you like to go on a vacation?"

Wilbur was quiet for a moment. "Who would water my garden while I was gone?"

"I hadn't thought of that," said Mili. But Wilbur didn't seem to hear her. He had disappeared to reach for a weed.

Mili went back to her apartment. She took out the picture of the *Mona Lisa.* Then she picked up her paints, a canvas, and an easel and went outside again.

She set up her things in a sunny spot on the lawn. She taped the picture of the *Mona Lisa* to the easel and traced the shapes onto her canvas. As she worked, she forgot about her map. She forgot about her busy friends. She forgot about her photo album and all the places she'd been before.

She thought about the light that made Mona Lisa's face look so soft, the gentle way she folded her paws, and her peaceful eyes.

Mili painted for hours. The sun hung low behind the oak tree. When she stood up to get a look at her work, she had the feeling she wasn't alone. She turned around to discover Wilbur, Emma, Violet, Fernando, and Henry sitting behind her, their eyes glued to her painting.

"Who is that?" whispered Violet.

"That is the *Mona Lisa*," said Mili. "It's a famous painting in Paris, France."

"It's so beautiful," gasped Henry.

"I've never seen anything like it," said Wilbur.

"We should go see it!" Emma cried.

Mili's heart leapt.

The Sprout Street neighbors followed Mili back to her apartment. They read her travel guides. They looked on the calendar for a good day to leave. Then they picked up a tiny yellow pin from the cup and placed it on the map, right in the city of Paris.

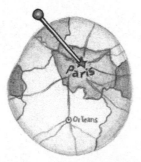

CHAPTER 2

Au Revoir

Henry reached into his dresser. He pulled out his best button-down shirt and some pinstriped pants. Then he placed them in the suitcase at the foot of his bed. He took his pencil and drew a check next to *Dinner clothes* on his Get Ready for Paris list.

Next on the list was *Snacks for the plane ride*. He chose a box of crackers and some banana chips in the kitchen and packed them next to his pants. He picked up the pencil again. *Check.*

He glanced at his pillow. The hotel couldn't possibly have pillows as comfortable as his. Perhaps he'd better bring it along. When he put it next to the banana chips, it filled up the bag. So he closed it and went to get another.

On the way he caught sight of his quilt. He could not imagine that a softer, warmer quilt existed in the world. Paris was likely to be chilly at night. He'd better take that along, too. Henry

placed it in the second suitcase. He added *Pillow* and *Quilt* to the list and drew two checks.

He was filling his fifth suitcase when there was a knock at the window. "What are you doing in there?" asked Violet, popping her head through.

Get Ready for Paris
✓1. Travel clothes
✓2. Pajamas
✓3. Dinner clothes
✓4. Snacks for the Plane ride
✓5. Pillow
✓6. Quilt
7. Shoes

Henry looked up from his list. "Packing," he said. "Trips take planning and hard work." Henry hadn't actually gotten ready for a trip before, but he felt he knew what he was talking about.

Violet looked at the growing stack of bags. "How will you carry all those things to the airport?" she asked.

Henry headed into the living room. "Can't talk now," he called out. "Have to pack my shoes!"

On the way he spied his bookshelf. He would need something to read on the airplane. So he pulled out a short book of poetry. "Will this last the whole flight?" he wondered. He put three more volumes in his bag. "Come to think of it," said Henry out loud, "I am a fast reader." So he packed up all his books.

"It is very hard to read without enough light," he continued. So Henry packed his reading lamp. "It is very uncomfortable to read without a reading chair and a rug underfoot," he went on. So he pushed them into the middle of the room and wrapped them in brown paper and twine.

Soon Henry's apartment was nearly empty, with a large pile of suitcases and furniture in the middle. His list was long and had many checks. Henry felt ready. But his apartment felt lonely.

Would it miss him when he was thousands of miles away?

Henry went for a walk to clear his head. Outside, puffy cotton clouds floated behind leafy branches. A blue jay hopped out of its nest and into the sky. Henry gazed at the empty nest bobbing on the branch, waiting for the bird to return.

All at once, Henry ran back to his apartment. Bursting through his door, he shouted, "I'm not going anywhere! This is where I belong-long-long!" His voice echoed off the bare walls.

Henry threw his jacket onto the floor and reached for his bags to unpack. But the pile wasn't there. Henry blinked. Had he put his things in the bedroom? He went into the next room, but there was nothing in there, either.

Henry's heart thumped loudly in his chest. "My warm quilt," he whimpered, "my comfortable pillow, my beautiful books . . ." Henry turned around and around, looking for a sign of his things.

"Is everything okay-ay-ay?" called a voice behind him. Wilbur came into the room and stood next to Henry. "I saw you run by-by-by," said Wilbur. "Where is all your stuff-uff-uff?"

"I don't know-ow-ow," said Henry.

Wilbur studied the apartment.

Then he tapped Henry on the arm and pointed to the door. By the entrance was a piece of twine on the ground. The friends walked over to it.

Wilbur peered through the door and noticed something else. In the hallway he saw some brown paper, stuck to the welcome mat.

Henry picked up the piece

of paper and looked through the  window. There lay a roll of packing tape on the stoop.

Henry looked at Wilbur. Wilbur looked at Henry. Then they went outside and followed the strange trail all the way down Sprout Street to Elm.

By the curb in front of the post office was Violet's bike trailer, full of Henry's things. Henry threw open the door. *Jing-a-ling* went the bell.

Violet peeked out from behind a large box she was carrying. "Oh, hi, Henry. Surprise! I am shipping all your things to Paris so they'll be there when we arrive."

"NO!" shouted Henry.

Violet jumped.

"You can't! I mean, please don't! I'm not going

on the trip. I made a mistake. My things belong at 24 Sprout Street and so do I."

Violet blinked. "You belong with us."

"If I go with you, my apartment will be all alone," said Henry.

Violet blinked again. "If you say so," she said, lowering the box onto the counter.

Violet, Henry, and Wilbur loaded everything back into the bike trailer. They returned to 24 Sprout Street and brought Henry's things inside.

"Thanks anyway, Violet," said Henry.

His friends closed the door behind them. Too tired to unpack, Henry just climbed into his bed and fell asleep.

The next morning, he noticed a small red envelope on the floor by the front door. The card said *Thinking of You* on the outside, and inside was a note that read:

Thinking of you

Dear Pillow,

Henry will come back soon, if he goes to Paris, and sleep on you right away. The fluffy pillows at the hotel will do in the meantime. Don't worry!

All the best,
Violet

Henry pulled his pillow out of his suitcase and placed it on the bed, next to the card.

Soon after, another envelope appeared under the door. On the outside it said *You Are the Best*, and on the inside it read:

Dear Books,

Henry loves to read you and will pick you up again shortly. While he is gone, he will read maps, street signs, and menus in Paris. But he will always think of you.

Sincerely,
Violet

Henry smiled and set his beautiful books neatly on the shelf.

Before long, another card appeared. On the outside it read *You're on My Mind,* and on the inside was another note:

Dear Quilt,

You are so soft and snug. Henry cannot wait to climb underneath you when he returns from Paris. Until then, you will warm his dreams.

Yours,
Violet

Henry took his quilt out of the suitcase and gave it the card. Then he put the rest of his things back in their place, save for two small suitcases filled with clothes and snacks.

He opened a card and began to write. On the outside it said *Thank You,* and on the inside it read:

Dear Violet,

You are right. I belong with you. And my home will wait patiently for me here. I'll meet you at the bus in the morning.

Your friend,
Henry

CHAPTER 3

Takeoff

The bus to the airport shut its doors and pulled away from the curb. It took off down Sprout Street, barreling out of town. Emma sat in the back. As the bus bumped along, she bounced up and down like a basketball. Her neighbors sat ahead of her, holding on to their seats.

With each bump, Emma raised her paws and went sailing. She gasped with joy, landed briefly on the seat cushion, then flew up into the air again.

She couldn't decide which was more thrilling—bouncing on the bus or the plane ticket in her pocket.

As they careened on to Cedar Hill Road, the luggage rack above Emma quivered. The bus hit a pothole, and a large suitcase fell, *ka-dunk-a-dunk-dunk,* its contents skittering across the floor.

Wilbur turned around. "Are you okay back there?"

Emma lunged for the bag. "My suitcase!" she cried.

Wilbur and Violet got down on all fours with Emma and grabbed what they could reach.

"I have your flashlight!" called Wilbur.

"Here is your camera!" Violet added.

Mili reached under her seat and picked up a large telescope with a crack through the glass. "What is this for?" she asked.

"Sightseeing—or at least it was!" said Emma. Suddenly the bus screeched to a stop, and the telescope flew out of Mili's paw. Emma slid forward. A duffel bag from the luggage rack catapulted through the air and rolled onto the floor next to her.

The bus driver turned to see what was going on. Emma looked up at him and smiled. "Are we there yet?"

"You have to stay in your seat," said the driver, helping her up.

Emma trotted back to her spot. Her friends sat down as well.

When they arrived at the airport, Henry, Violet, Wilbur, Mili, Fernando, and Emma gathered her things, picked up their bags, and stepped outside. The sun beamed down as they paraded through security to gate 89.

Emma skipped along behind Fernando, watching the gate numbers. Gate 62. Gate 74. With each number she passed, her heart rose like a seat on a Ferris wheel. Finally, she could bear it no longer. She took off at full speed toward their gate, passing everyone, bags flying out behind her. She looked to her right. Gate 89!

Emma tried to stop in time. But the airport floor was slippery. Her bags knocked her off balance, and she dove onto the ground.

"Look out!" cried Fernando, pointing at a magazine stand.

The Sprout Street neighbors watched Emma roll like a bowling ball into a magazine display. *Tha-KUNK-A-BOOM.* Magazines flew in all directions, and one of Emma's bags burst open again. This time, plastic fruit spilled out, making the airport look like the produce section at Sergio's.

Emma sat on the floor, in a pile of plastic apples, bananas, and strawberries. Above her, a clerk shook her head and put her paws on her hips.

Fernando ran over and helped Emma up. "So sorry!" he told the clerk, grabbing the magazines and holding them to his chest. "I'll take all of these."

Emma stuffed her things back inside her bag.

"Why did you bring plastic fruit?" asked Fernando.

"They go on my opera hat," replied Emma. "It must have fallen apart when I fell."

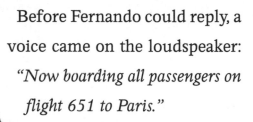

Before Fernando could reply, a voice came on the loudspeaker: *"Now boarding all passengers on flight 651 to Paris."*

Emma's eyes got as big

as dinner plates. "It's time!" she cried.

Fernando rushed to the register to pay for the magazines. Then he and Emma hurried back to gate 89.

"Come on!" shouted Mili, gesturing with her paw toward the ramp.

Emma followed her friends into the plane. She hopped up and down in the aisle, looking for her seat. Through the tiny windows, Emma could see the wings outside stretching long into the horizon.

Row 15. Row 22. Row 31. At last, Emma found her seat. She lifted her suitcases overhead and pushed them into a bin. But when she tried to close the door, the bags got in the way.

"Here, let me help you," said Wilbur. He held on to the door and pulled it down with all his might.

Riiiiip. The door tore into Emma's suitcase, and her bag exploded once more. The passengers were covered in a shower of Emma's things. Fernando's ears wore pajama pants. A hula hoop circled Mili's feet. And Henry jumped with surprise when a homing pigeon burst from the bag and landed on his shoulder.

The bird flapped its wings, crying, *"Woo woo, woo woo!"*

"Help!" shouted Henry, standing on his seat and waving his paws in the air.

"Come here, Frances!" called Emma, reaching out her arm. Frances took to the air and landed gently on Emma's wrist.

"You can't bring pigeons on a plane!" shouted Henry.

"What if we need to send a message home from Paris?" asked Emma.

A flight attendant rushed over. "I'm afraid you'll have to leave your bird at the airport."

Emma's face fell. "Do you promise to take good care of her?"

"We will," said the flight attendant. "Come pick her up at the information desk when you return."

Emma handed over Frances, stuffed the rest of her things back in the bin, and collapsed in her seat. For the first time that day, Emma was still. Her visions of sending postcards home with Frances, dressing grandly for the theater, and peering at Paris through her telescope were disappearing faster than the ground beneath them as the plane rose into the air. "The trip is ruined," said Emma.

"Don't worry," replied Mili, sitting in the seat next to her. "All a traveler really needs are a map and a good friend."

"I don't have a map," said Emma.

"I do," said Mili. She pulled one out of her bag and unfolded it on their laps.

The map was covered in red marker where Mili had circled the places she wanted to go. "This is the Eiffel Tower," she began. "You can take an elevator to the top and see the whole city. You don't even need a telescope!" Emma leaned in to get a better look.

"Over here is the Marais, a beautiful neighborhood for getting snacks and buying mementos. I'm sure they will have postcards for you to send to Frances.

"This river is called the Seine," she went on. "We can take an evening cruise here." Mili pointed to a dock on the river.

Emma shifted in her seat. "What should I wear?" she asked.

"Let me see," said Mili. She pulled a banana out of her bag and put it on Emma's head.

Emma picked it up, peeled it, and took a bite. "Delicious," she giggled. And the friends laughed all the way to Paris.

CHAPTER 4

Bonjour

Fernando looked in the mirror of his hotel room and cleared his throat. He glanced at his French phrase book, then back at his reflection. "BAWN-joooor!" he said, pursing his lips. He took a breath and tried again. "BUN-jurrr!"

Fernando shook his head and frowned. "That can't be right," he said out loud. He had been in Paris for two days and hadn't spoken to anyone but his friends. While they had breakfast in the lobby, Fernando stayed in his room and worried.

He walked over to the window and peeked out at the shoppers strolling below. One looked up and waved. *"Salut!"* she called out.

Fernando ducked back inside the hotel room as fast as he could. "Did she just call me Saloo?" he gasped.

Emma burst through the door. *"BONJOUR,* Fernando!"

"It's Saloo," said Fernando, looking at his shoes.

"It's both," said Emma. "*Salut* AND *bonjour* mean 'hello' in French." She skipped over to her dresser and rifled through her things, pulling out a scarf covered in purple sequins.

"Everyone is headed to the river today," she said, wrapping the scarf around her neck. "But I was thinking of taking a walk. Would you like to join me?"

"Weeey," said Fernando.

Emma giggled and put on her backpack. "*Yes* is pronounced *wee* in French, Fernando."

They went downstairs and headed outside. The birds hopped from branch to branch and sang. *Chi-eep chi-eep!* Fernando wondered what that might mean in English. He turned to ask

Emma, but she was a few yards ahead, looking through the window of a cheese shop.

Turning back to the sidewalk, he spotted a tall fellow walking toward him with a red velvet hat on his head. The band was embroidered with lilies. Its gold stitching shone in the morning sun. It was the most beautiful hat Fernando had ever seen. He couldn't take his eyes off it.

The man stopped in front of him. *"Bonjour,"* he said, nodding.

Fernando stopped, too. "Saloo," he said softly.

"Vous aimez mon chapeau?" said the man.

Fernando panicked. What did he say? It sounded like he was talking about shampoo. *"Shampoo?"* repeated Fernando.

The man furrowed his brow. He nodded again and walked away.

"French people must like shampoo," he said to Emma. But she didn't answer. She was gone again. And she wasn't ahead of him, either. Fernando turned around and around, but Emma was no-where to be seen.

His face got hot, and his ears burned red. How would he find his way without her? Which way was the hotel again? What was French for *I'm lost*?

There was a tap on his shoulder. He looked behind him to find a shopkeeper who had come outside.

"*Votre ami est parti?*" he asked.

Fernando blinked. Party? Did the clerk think he was going to a party? Why would he go to a party when he couldn't find Emma!

Fernando turned around and ran. He hoped it was in the direction of the hotel, but he couldn't be sure. He ran past the cheese shop and the man with the velvet hat. He ran and ran and ran, until he couldn't run anymore.

When he stopped to catch his breath, he was in the middle of a park. He sat down on a bench, next to an accordion player. The musician was pulling his instrument in and out, out and in. It looked like a caterpillar climbing across a leaf. His feet flew over the keys and made a sound Fernando had never heard before. The music was not in English or French, but it spoke to him.

Three dancers spun out from behind a fountain and made a circle. They moved their arms up and down as they danced, their skirts spinning wide like flower petals. Fernando was too surprised to speak, but he didn't have to. He closed his eyes. The music drifted over him, and he didn't feel lost anymore.

"*Dansons?*"

He could have sworn he heard the word *dance*.

"*Dansons?*"

Fernando opened his eyes and saw one of the dancers bending low in front of him, reaching out her arm.

"Dance?" asked Fernando. The dancer nodded. He couldn't believe it. She understood him.

He understood her. He was speaking French! Or she was speaking English? He wasn't sure, but he didn't care.

Fernando stood up and took her hand. Together they twirled and swayed, lifting their arms like tree branches in the wind.

He closed his eyes again, taking in the sound. When he opened them, the park was full of dancers, everyone moving to the music. He felt a tap on his shoulder for the second time that day. But this time when he turned around, he knew just what to say.

"Emma!" he cried.

"Fernando!" sang Emma. "I've been looking for you everywhere!"

Emma and Fernando joined paws and danced until the song was finished. Slowly, the

park cleared. Fernando walked over to the accordion player and dropped a coin in his hat.

"Merci," said the accordion player.

Fernando smiled. He knew just what he
meant.

CHAPTER 5

The Portrait

Wilbur put his train pass into the machine in the Paris Métro entrance. When his ticket popped out again, he plucked it from the slot and went through the turnstile. The doors in front of him opened like magic. *WHOOSH*. He stepped between them and onto the platform to wait for the train with Fernando.

On the wall was a sprawling map. Wilbur and Fernando let their eyes wander over the squiggly lines that looked like the edges of a puzzle piece. Tiny dots were spaced along them, marking the train stations: Oberkampf, Pigalle, Varenne, Belleville.

"I wonder if it gets noisy in Belleville?" asked Fernando, nudging Wilbur with his elbow.

Wilbur chuckled. "I don't know, but I bet they like to eat bell-oney!"

"That doesn't ring a bell!" cried Fernando.

Wilbur and Fernando laughed and laughed. Then, suddenly, the ground started to shake. A train pulled up to the platform, and the friends went inside.

In minutes, they were speeding through the Paris underground. The train car rocked from side to side as it flew through the dark tunnel. Wilbur imagined plants growing in the ground over their heads. Did their roots turn and twist in the earth? Could the leaves that sprouted above them feel the train humming underneath?

Fernando looked at a poster on the wall of the train. "JAR-daan day PLONT," said Fernando, carefully reading the words at the top. "Is that where we're going?"

Wilbur nodded. "I think you're really getting the hang of French!"

"I've been practicing," said Fernando.

At the next stop, Fernando and Wilbur walked out into a world of green. Blossoms lined the sidewalk, dressed in bright red and orange uniforms.

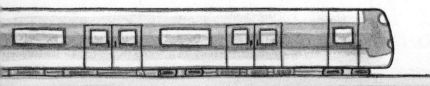

Wilbur smelled the sweet spring air as they made their way to the garden's entrance and bought two tickets.

"I read there is a glass greenhouse inside," said Wilbur.

Fernando had never seen a greenhouse before. He followed his friend through the gates.

They turned a corner and stopped in their tracks. In front of them was a parade of leafy animals, marching across the lawn. Branches

formed floppy ears, arching necks, and tails swinging through the air.

"I didn't realize we were going to the zoo!" said Fernando.

Wilbur squinted his eyes. He could just make out the winding wooden trunks under each creature, connecting them to the ground. Could these be trees? Nothing on Sprout Street looked like this! He spotted a plaque nearby. It read *Topiary Garden*.

"Hey, Wilbur," said Fernando, pointing at a leafy dog chasing its tail, "what kind of tree do you think that is?"

"I'm not sure," Wilbur answered.

"A *dogwood*!" Fernando grinned.

Wilbur smiled and cleared his throat. Then he pointed to a tree shaped like a cat. "Fernando, why is that cat like a dog?"

Fernando waited.

"Because it's covered with *bark!*"

Fernando slapped his knee and shook with laughter. "I know, I know," he said, turning toward the jungle animals. "What did that giraffe say to the elephant who stepped on his toe?"

"What?" asked Wilbur.

"*Leaf* me alone!" cried Fernando, gasping for air.

Then he saw it. And he stopped laughing. "Look!" he whispered, pointing ahead.

"Is there a *tree* lion swimming over there?" giggled Wilbur. But when he turned the corner, he stopped laughing, too.

Wilbur's eyes moved from the trunk to the leaves to the top of a small tree. He began to get a familiar feeling, the feeling of looking in a mirror. Before him grew a tree, cut to look just like him.

"It's like they knew you were coming," whispered Fernando.

Wilbur could not imagine that anyone knew he was coming. A couple of weeks ago, he didn't even know himself.

He walked slowly around the Wilbur tree. It had a pair of clippers in one paw and a watering can in the other. It wore an apron and slip-on gardening shoes, like the ones Wilbur kept in his apartment at 24 Sprout Street.

Just then, a large ceramic pot came rolling into view from behind a hedge. *"Reviens ici!"* cried a frantic gardener, following close behind. The pot whizzed down the walkway, past Wil-

bur's feet. But the gardener did not. When his eyes fell on Wilbur, he forgot all about the pot. *"Te voilà!"* he cried, putting his hands on his hips.

"Bonjour," Wilbur offered, having no idea what the gardener had said.

"Bonjour?" said the gardener, looking confused.

Wilbur didn't know what to say, so he just nodded.

"I think he knows you," said Fernando.

The gardener turned and headed down the path, motioning with his paw for them to follow. Wilbur and Fernando looked at each other. Then they walked down the path after him. This day was getting stranger by the minute.

When they got to the end of the path, the gardener threw open the door to the greenhouse and walked inside. Wilbur and Fernando went in after him. The air was thick and wet. Sunlight bathed the plants surrounding them. Wilbur felt at home, even though he was miles away from Sprout Street.

A group of gardeners rushed toward him.

"Ici, mettez cela sur," said a tall gardener wearing an apron. He put one just like it over Wilbur's head and led everyone to the back of the greenhouse.

They stopped in a clearing where there were no tables. Before them was a large, overgrown tree, sitting in a pot.

Wilbur looked at the tree. But everyone else seemed to be staring at him. The tall gardener handed him some clippers. Wilbur now looked even more like the Wilbur tree. Except he was not where he was supposed to be.

"Excuse me," Wilbur spoke up, "I think there has been a mistake."

The gardeners looked at each other. Then they pointed at the tree.

Fernando cleared his throat. "Wilbur, I think they want you to cut it."

"I don't know how," whispered Wilbur.

"Sure you do—you garden all the time," Fernando whispered back.

"Not like *this*," he replied.

"Hey, Wilbur," said Fernando, "do you think they grow any plums in here? Because it seems like they really like to *prune*."

Wilbur looked at Fernando and smiled. He stepped closer to the tree and opened the clippers. First, he cut off a few stray branches. On the sides he began to make a round shape, and on the top, two tall points. He worked slowly, one snip at a time.

"Hello," said someone behind him.

Wilbur turned around and dropped his clippers. Once again, he felt like he was looking in the mirror. But this time, his image wasn't covered in green leaves.

Wilbur and the stranger walked in a circle, looking each other up and down. The stranger had the same pointy ears, the same gray stripes in his fur, and the same pink nose. They could have been cousins. "You speak English?" asked Wilbur.

"Yes," he said. "Lots of people in Paris do. My name is Alphonse. I make the topiary in the garden. I was running late to work today. It looks like you started my job for me!"

Wilbur nodded.

"Did you see my self-portrait outside?"

Wilbur nodded again. Everything was starting to make sense.

Alphonse looked at the tree, then at Wilbur, then over at Fernando. "Here, let me help you," said Alphonse.

He picked up the clippers and got to work. "Like this," he said, showing Wilbur how he held them close to the plant. "Start by cutting big shapes; after that you make smaller ones."

Alphonse and Wilbur took turns clipping the tree, while Fernando sat on an overturned pot and watched. The sun began to sink low outside. At last, they stood back to admire their work. *"Voilà!"* shouted Alphonse.

Fernando looked at his portrait. His cheeks turned as pink as the sunset. "It's me!" Fernando gasped. "I'm a work of art!"

"I thought the Wilbur tree could use some company," said Wilbur.

The two friends said their goodbyes and headed back toward the train station. "No one is going to believe us," said Fernando as they strolled down the busy sidewalk.

"That's okay," said Wilbur. "I will never forget."

CHAPTER 6

The Masterpiece

Mona Lisa smiled at Violet from inside a shiny golden frame. Violet stared back from behind a rope, her neighbors by her side. Fernando held up a camera and snapped pictures. Emma hopped on her toes, trying to get a better look. Wilbur was as still as a statue, his hands in his pockets. And Henry studied what he saw, then scribbled wildly in his notebook.

"Was she real?" Violet whispered to Mili.

"It's a mystery," Mili whispered back. "But

we think her name was Lisa. The artist Leonardo da Vinci painted her portrait. She inspired him."

Mili looked like she was a million miles away. But the crowd around them was closer than ever. Violet felt an elbow poking her wing. Someone tripped and fell against her backpack. The room began to feel like an oven. So Violet squeezed through the sea of cameras until she was free.

The halls of the Louvre lay before her like a vast maze. Violet wandered the museum slowly, looking for a place to draw. The walls reached high overhead like trees in a forest. The ceiling above her was painted in clouds. Art was everywhere. There were portraits of ladies under feathery hats and noble kings waving their swords. Gold vines wound their way up marble columns and looped over doorways like twinkle lights at Christmas.

Violet climbed a long stairway to a room with a round window in the ceiling. Beneath it was a statue in a flowing dress, balanced on the prow of a ship. Wings reached out behind her, as if she were about to take flight. But the head and arms were missing.

Violet read the name on a plaque nearby: Winged Victory of Samothrace. The statue was made to celebrate a victory at sea.

"What happened to her head?" Violet wondered out loud.

"We don't know," said a voice out of nowhere. "She is very old. It probably broke off."

Violet looked over her shoulder and saw someone drawing on an easel. "Thanks," said Violet. "What are you drawing?"

"The statue," said the artist. "She inspires me."

Violet sat down on a step and took out her notebook. Maybe she would feel inspired, too. Maybe the Winged Victory would send her pencil flying across the page, like Henry's did. But when she opened the book, her mind went blank. So she closed it again and kept walking.

The walls around her were bursting with stories. Crowded ships bobbed along bumpy oceans. Horses galloped through the air. Cas-

tles sat on mountaintops.
People in long, fancy
robes had mysterious
looks on their faces.

From across the room,
something caught her
eye. Her feet clicked against the marble floor,
klip-klop, klip-klop, as she went to get a closer
look.

On the wall hung the strangest painting she

had ever seen. The lips were
made of tiny rosebuds, the
ears were blooming peonies,
and at the top of the head
grew a perfect white lily.
"Wilbur would love this,"
she said to herself, as happy
as a summer garden.

But then she thought of her notebook and her smile faded like a blossom in November. She had never painted a face of flowers, a great victory at sea, or someone as important as Mona Lisa. Nothing even close.

"There you are!" shouted a voice behind her. Mili ran to her side. "We were looking all over for you. Want to go eat lunch? Everyone is waiting outside."

Violet followed Mili out into the sun. The courtyard was busy and full. They bought two crepes at a food cart and sat down next to Fernando, Wilbur, Emma, and Henry.

Mili was grinning from ear to

ear. "I can't wait to go home and paint!"

Fernando piped up, "Hey, Mili, what is an artist's favorite way to swim?"

"I don't know—what?" replied Mili.

"The brushstroke!" cried Fernando. Everyone burst out laughing. All except for Henry, who was bent over a postcard. He was writing to his apartment about everything they'd seen on their last day in Paris.

Emma was next to him, sorting the trinkets she'd bought in the gift shop. "The Eiffel Tower key chain is for Sergio, the chocolates are for Mr. Ashby, and the tiny beret is for Frances."

Emma turned to Violet. "Are you bringing anything home with you?"

"I wanted to make a drawing," said Violet, "but my notebook is empty."

"Just look around and find something that inspires you," said Mili.

Violet let her eyes wander through the courtyard. Sunlight gleamed off the glass pyramid nearby. Water fountains sprayed into the air, then splashed down into sparkling pools. Beyond them, the city of Paris stretched out, full of gardens, musicians, art, and museums.

She looked at Mili, Henry, Emma, Fernando, and Wilbur. She thought about getting on the airplane together in the morning and flying over the wide ocean between France and 24 Sprout Street. All of a sudden, she realized she didn't need to take anything home. But she did want to leave something there.

She picked up a pencil and traced the shape of

their apartment building. She drew the porch at the bottom, the windows in the middle, and the roof garden on top. In the yard, she drew her friends writing, painting, dancing, and gardening.

Before they went back to the train, she made one last visit to a large, grand hall, filled with the most famous artwork in the world. And she left behind a little piece of home.

A Glossary of French Terms in the Story

au revoir (oh reh-VWAH): good-bye, or until we meet again

bonjour (bohn-ZHOOR): hello, or good day

Dansons (dahn-SOHN): Let's dance, or Dance.

Ici, mettez cela sur (ee-SEE meh-TAY SEH-lah soor): Here, put this on.

Jardin des Plantes (ZHAR-dahn day plahnt): The largest botanical garden in France. Its name means "garden of plants."

Le Marais (leh muh-RAY): A historic district in Paris. Its name means "the marsh."

Louvre (LOO-vruh): A world-famous art museum in central Paris. It's the largest museum in the world.

merci (mehr-SEE): thank you

oui (wee): yes

Reviens ici! (REH-vee-ehn ee-SEE): Come back here!

salut (sah-LOO): hello, or greetings

Seine (sehn): A river that flows through Paris.

Te voilà (tuh VWUH-lah): There you are.

Voilà! (VWUH-lah): Here it is! or This is it! or Here!

Votre ami est parti? (VOH-truh ah-MEE ay par-TEE): Your friend is gone? or Did your friend leave?

Vous aimez mon chapeau? (vooz eh-MAY mohn shaa-POH): Do you like my hat?